13 ALABAMA GHOSTS
and Jeffrey

13 Alabama Ghosts
and Jeffrey
COMMEMORATIVE EDITION

Kathryn Tucker Windham
Margaret Gillis Figh

With a New Afterword by
Dilcy Windham Hilley and Ben Windham

THE UNIVERSITY OF ALABAMA PRESS
Tuscaloosa

The University of Alabama Press
Tuscaloosa, Alabama 35487-0380
uapress.ua.edu

Hardcover edition published 2014.
Paperback edition published 2016.
eBook edition published 2014.

Inquiries about reproducing material from this work should be
addressed to the University of Alabama Press.

Typeface: Times New Roman

Photographs by Kathryn Tucker Windham (unless otherwise indicated)
Cover art illustrations by Delores Eskins Atkins
Cover design: Delores Eskins Atkins

Paperback ISBN: 978-0-8173-5882-2

Cataloging-in-Publication data is available from
the Library of Congress.
ISBN: 978-0-8173-1842-0 (cloth)
ISBN: 978-0-8173-8705-1 (electronic)

Contents

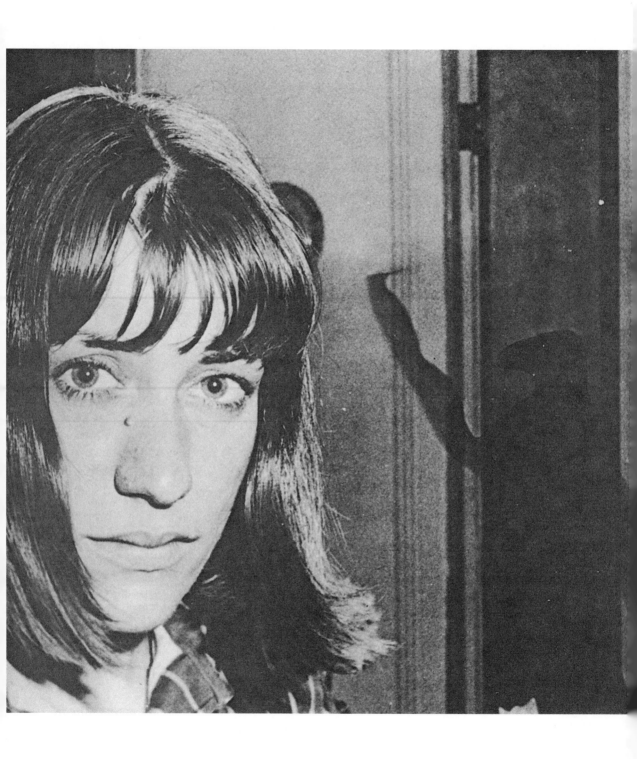

Jeffrey, right, with his live female companion, Nikki.

Foreword

Frankly, until we saw the photograph of Jeffrey (shown on opposite page) we were skeptical about ghosts. We also were skeptical about ghost books. If anyone besides our reliable and reputable author, Kathryn Tucker Windham, had brought us this photograph, our skepticism would have continued to be spirited, shall we say. Kathryn has been writing for us since her first edition of *Treasured Alabama Recipes* in 1964, and we have come to know her as an earthy and trustworthy friend. So when she maintained, with an eager and genuine south-Alabama expression, that she now owned a house ghost and that here was a photograph of him or her or it, well we borrowed the photograph and asked permission to give it the "third degree."

We began by requesting a reputable art consultant, the Ludwig Studios of Cherry Hill, New Jersey, to give the photograph a controlled and detailed study. Ludwig's photography staff spent several months analyzing Jeffrey by means of technical tests. They performed a series of actual experiments to see if darkroom shenanigans in the first place could have transposed Jeffrey's photograph onto the negative. All to no avail. They could not conjure up an artificial Jeffrey no matter how many photographic tricks they tried. Jeffrey remained not only unsurpassed—he remained unduplicated.

Next we checked out the girl photographed with Jeffrey. Her name is Nikki Davis, and she is a staff photographer for the *Selma Times-Journal* in Selma, Alabama. From a small farming community in Mississippi, she too has a reputation for integrity and honesty. She is photographed with Jeffrey because she, along with several friends, was visiting her newspaper coworker Kathryn Windham one evening when they decided to make photographs in Kathryn's house. They shot two rolls of films that evening. The next day Nikki was developing them casually at the *Selma Times-Journal* when suddenly, Nikki says, "I almost overturned the developing tank." One of the prints she was developing showed a ghost!

Startled by her discovery Nikki and her friends returned quickly to Kathryn's home to check for possible causes for the photographic image. They tried to see if a shadow might have caused it, so they made more photographs duplicating, wherever possible, conditions of the previous evening. They made one photograph from the same angle that had caught Jeffrey the previous go-round. But Jeffrey was camera shy at this second taking.

Kathryn Windham and her former English teacher, Margaret Gillis Figh of Huntingdon College in Montgomery, Alabama, have gone out of their way to be neutral concerning Jeffrey and the thirteen other ghosts in this book. "We're not asking anyone to become ghost believers," they point out. "We have simply tried to report these stories as honestly and as accurately as we can." Between them they have conjured a heady brew. They hope that everyone stirs it with his own choice of broomstick, but no one is asked to heap his bowl with what he neither needs nor desires.

When the two authors completed this ghost book, Kathryn suggested that we meet her in Decatur, Alabama, at a statewide conference of the Alabama Associated Press. So we went to Decatur, and she handed us a notebook containing an original and a carbon of this ghost chronicle. We suggested that Kathryn jot down her own explanation of Jeffrey and this book, to be included with the Foreword.

This she did later that night in longhand on motel stationery, which she mailed to us the next morning. We are pleased to include it:

This book is dedicated to Jeffrey whose picture appears earlier.

Jeffrey took up residence at the Windham home in Selma about three years ago. The family first became aware of his presence when they would hear someone moving around in the living room or clumping down the hall. But nobody was ever there.

They might have decided sound waves were playing tricks on them had it not been for the reaction of their cat, an old and respected feline known as Hornblower; he heard the noises too. Whenever the family heard the footsteps, Hornblower would jump up (even rousing from a sound sleep), arch his back, and flex his claws. The hair around his neck would stand in a stiff ruff as he prepared to spring at an unseen but disturbing presence.

Jeffrey usually confines his activities to stomping up and down the hall, stirring around in the living room, shaking lamps, and setting empty chairs to rocking; but on at least two occasions he has moved objects.

The first thing he moved was a heavy chest of drawers which he shoved three or four inches alongside a wall until the chest blocked the door. That door, which was closed at the time, is the only entrance into the room, and it could not be opened until the barricading chest was moved by pushing with great force against the door.

That same week a cake baked for a friend was placed on the dining table while a hurried search for car keys was underway. During the search for the keys, which lasted only about three minutes, Jeffrey moved the cake over on the table so that it was about to fall onto the floor. One more small push would have upset its balance and spilled it. Nobody was in the house at the time except the cake maker—and Jeffrey.

Then one night, when Jeffrey had not given evidence of his presence for several weeks, some young people had been playing with a ouija board and making a table talk. The conversation, naturally, included references to Jeffrey. During the evening the group took several pictures of one another, using standard film and flash equipment. Next day when the pictures were developed and printed, there was Jeffrey.

The photographic work was done in the darkroom at the Selma Times-Journal by a staff photographer who was more surprised and mystified than anybody else by the strange image on the print. The eerie, shadowy thing, whatever it is, appears to have posed for the portrait.

Soon after Jeffrey had his picture made (which is believed to be the only instance of a ghost providing a picture of himself for a writer of ghost stories), the Windhams decided to consult with Margaret Gillis Figh of Montgomery, Alabama, about the ghost at their house. Mrs. Figh, an authority on folklore, has collected ghost stories for many years.

Out of that consultation grew this book, a collection of stories not about Jeffrey but about thirteen of Alabama's other famous ghosts.

You, the reader, please note: we have called upon the spirits at our command in visibly, rather than invisibly, printing Kathryn's letter in this Foreword. THE STRODE PUBLISHERS

Preface

Alabama has many ghosts.

Stop in almost any town in the state and if you inquire around, the chances are that you will find a ghost story.

Old residents will point out a dilapidated structure known locally as a haunted house or will give you directions to a run-down decaying mansion or to the overgrown site where once stood "the grandest plantation house in the county"—a real haunted house.

Unhappily, most of the tales about these places and the specters that haunt them are fragmentary and repetitious, consisting mainly of vague accounts of mysterious footsteps, slamming doors, clanking chains, or darting lights. But there are Alabama ghosts of distinction whose marvelous exploits have entertained many generations of listeners and who have become a treasured part of Southern folklore.

Thirteen of these stories have been selected for use in this book. Some readers may find that the versions of tales in this collection differ from the stories they have heard. Since these stories have been handed down by word of mouth, it is to be expected that there should be differences. We have tried to record the versions which are most complete and which best portray the traditional lore.

One aim of this volume is to preserve pictures of the fast disappearing old houses and other spots which these revenants have haunted, but its major purpose is to record tales of those spirits whose adventures have had such widespread appeal that they may be designated as Alabama's greatest ghosts.

A rutted clay road leads across a rocky pasture, skirts a clump of tall cedars, and ends at the foot of an overgrown knoll.

The Ghost of The Angry Architect

 HE BARBED WIRE GATE HAS
a rusty "No Trespassing" sign
stapled to it. Beyond the gate a
rutted clay road leads across a
rocky pasture, skirts a clump of
tall cedars, and ends at the foot
of an overgrown knoll.

On the top of that promontory once stood Rocky Hill
Castle, the showplace of the Tennessee River Valley area.

So imposing was its architecture—or so remote was
its location—that Rocky Hill Castle escaped the fate of
many of the other antebellum mansions in that area during
the final months of the Civil War: deliberate burning by
Federal troops. However, neglect and vandalism combined
to destroy Rocky Hill Castle, leaving only a pile of rubble
and a long, silent avenue of cedars to mark the spot where
the castle stood.

Rocky Hill Castle was the kind of house that invited—
even required—ghosts. And the ghosts were there almost
from the time Rocky Hill Castle was completed.

13

In 1832 twenty-six-year-old James E. Saunders moved from Brunswick County, Virginia, to Rocky Hill, three miles east of the established village of Courtland in Lawrence County, Alabama. Saunders was a lawyer, a former student at the University of Georgia. He had left the university at the age of eighteen to marry fifteen-year-old Mary Frances Watkins. Older people shook their heads and said, privately, that the couple was much too young for marriage. But James and Mary lived happily together for sixty-five years, many of those years at Rocky Hill Castle.

Nobody knows the exact date that Rocky Hill Castle was built, but it was probably in the late 1840's. By that time Saunders was an established lawyer, prominent in the politics of the state, a member of the legislature, the head of a growing family, and the owner of thousands of acres of rich Tennessee River land. He was a proud man, and he wanted a home grand enough for a man of his standing and position. So he built Rocky Hill Castle.

His architect came from France, bringing with him plans for the house's identical front and rear porticos with their fluted Doric columns, the graceful spiral staircase in the entrance hall, the ornate acanthus leaf decorative motifs, the arched windows in the cupola atop the roof.

Slaves on the Saunders plantation made the bricks for the mansion, shaping them from the red clay found on the place and firing them in the large kilns built for the purpose. The warm red color of the bricks did not show, however, since it was hidden beneath a heavy coating of stucco.

It was a magnificent house, so grand that even a man of James Saunders' wealth was not able to pay for it. When the architect presented his bill, Saunders was astonished at its size. Normally a restrained man, he lost his temper completely and shouted angry threats at the equally angry Frenchman.

The Frenchman departed, cursing the mansion and its "thieving master." Not long afterward he died, still resentful over never having been paid what he felt was due him for his work.

Thus the background was laid for the ghost of that artistic and indignant Frenchman to become the first of many spectral visitors to Rocky Hill Castle.

Sometimes at night when the Saunders family was seated at the long table in the dining room having an evening meal, or when gathered around the square piano in the music room for an informal musicale, loud noises of pounding were heard in the cellar as though someone were beating on the foundations with a heavy hammer.

When the pounding first started, braver members of the family would rush down to the cellar to investigate. But no matter how fast they ran or how thoroughly they searched, they never found anything unusual in the dark, silent cellar.

Then almost as soon as the searchers rejoined the rest of the family upstairs, the heavy thuds would begin again, seeming at times to shake the whole house.

The mysterious hammering continued almost as long as the Saunders family lived at Rocky Hill Castle, and eventually they became accustomed to the noise and even laughed in a rather subdued sort of way about the angry architect's apparition trying to destroy the mansion he had created by knocking it from its very foundations.

The French architect was not the only ghost to haunt Rocky Hill Castle.

Colonel Saunders supervised the construction of this turret, six stories tall, at one end of Rocky Hill Castle. (Photograph by Dudley Campbell)

Sometime after his classic home was completed, after his quarrel with the architect, Colonel Saunders supervised the construction of a turret, six stories tall, at one end of the house. The stark Gothic tower contrasted strangely with the gentle lines of the house, but the clash of architectural styles did not disturb Colonel Saunders at all. He delighted in his tower.

From the top of the structure Colonel Saunders could see the acres and acres of land he owned, and he could watch his slaves at work in the fields. His voice was so powerful he could stand in the tower and shout orders audible to crews working a mile or more away.

With the approach of the Yankee forces during the final phase of the Civil War, the tower served as a hiding place for the family jewels, just as it had served earlier as a hiding place for Confederate soldiers and scouts.

Some of the Confederates who came to Rocky Hill Castle for refuge were sick and wounded, and Mrs. Saunders converted the top floor of the turret into an emergency infirmary for their care. Two young soldiers whose names were never known died there and were buried in the Saunders family cemetery near the house.

Although the two soldiers themselves never returned to haunt Rocky Hill Castle, one of them is said to be responsible for the next apparition who came, the ghost of a lovely young Confederate lady. It is thought that one of the dead soldiers was her sweetheart and that she was looking for him.

She made her appearance after the Saunders were moving back into Rocky Hill Castle (they sold and repurchased the property three times) after a period of absence. While Colonel Saunders was supervising the unpacking of some belongings outside the house, Mrs. Saunders pushed open the front door and hurried inside to see if Rocky Hill

17

Even as she spoke, the lady vanished.

Castle was still as lovely as when she had last lived there.

She started up the stairway, eager to see again the panoramic view from her bedroom window, when she was startled by a lady standing on the stairs. The lady, dressed in soft blue, stood with one hand resting on the stair rail and the other hand gracefully lifting, ever so slightly, her full hoop skirt.

Recovering from her surprise at finding someone in the house, Mrs. Saunders regained her composure, remembered her manners, and held out her hand to welcome her unexpected guest.

"Good morning," Mrs. Saunders said graciously, "I am Mrs. Saun - - - -"

Even as she spoke, the lady vanished.

Mrs. Saunders knew her family would laugh at her and tease her about "seeing things" if she told them about the incident, but she could not possibly keep such a secret. They did laugh and they did tease, but they could not shake her conviction that she had seen a little lady in blue.

Colonel Saunders stopped his teasing a few days later when he also had an encounter with the lady in blue. He had gone down to the wine cellar to get a bottle of blackberry wine, and as he was crossing the shadowy room to the wine racks he glanced up and saw a lady in blue sitting on a box and smiling at him.

The colonel, known throughout the state as a cordial and courtly host, completely lost his poise. He backed up the steps, never taking his eyes off the blue-gowned lady, slammed the cellar door shut, locked it, and did not ever return for his wine again.

The family's final encounter with ghosts came one morning when Mrs. Saunders was preparing to take her bath. There had recently been a number of unexplained noises and other such manifestations of phantom visitations,

19

He backed up the stairs, never taking his eyes off the blue-gowned lady.

and Mrs. Saunders had become provoked over the continuing annoyances. She was standing by the walnut wardrobe trying to decide which dress she would put on when the irritating noise began again.

Mrs. Saunders was not frightened, just disgusted and impatient.

"If there's anybody there, speak up or forever hold your peace," she shouted in annoyance.

Back came the distinct reply, "Madam, I'm right here!"

The Saunders family sold the house and moved out in less than two hours!

"Judge! Judge! Come quick!! Your house is burning up!"

Death Lights in the Tower

UDGE! JUDGE! COME QUICK!!
Your house is burning up!"

The excited man beat upon the door of the old mansion, trying to rouse its sleeping occupants.

Inside the house, Judge W. G. Cochrane was awakened by the commotion, and he lay still for a moment trying to identify the noise.

"Oh, no. Not again!" he muttered sleepily. But he got out of bed, threw his robe around his shoulders, and went to answer the door.

"The tower room is blazing," the Negro gasped as the judge opened the door. "You can see the fire all over this end of town!"

"All right. Let's go investigate," Judge Cochrane replied.

Together they climbed the two flights of stairs to the square tower room, and Judge Cochrane threw open the door.

The room was dark—no flames, no sparks, no smouldering ashes, not even a wisp of smoke.

The visitor shook his head in disbelief and hurried for the stairs.

"But I seen it myself! I seen it myself!" he kept repeating as Judge Cochrane escorted him down the hall and out the back door.

"Thank you for being concerned," the judge said wearily. "Good night."

"How many times has it happened now?" Judge Cochrane asked himself as he climbed back into bed. "And when will she stop burning those damnable candles?"

The "she" he referred to was Mrs. Sarah Drish, builder and longtime resident of what is now known as the Old Drish Place in Tuscaloosa. Mrs. Drish was a gentle, intelligent woman, but, according to tales told about her home, it is her frustrated ghost who returns to alarm the neighborhood by burning candles in the tower, candles which she wanted to be burned around her coffin at her death.

The story goes back to 1817 when three or four Owen brothers and their sister, Mrs. Sarah McKinney, a widow, came from Norfolk District, Virginia, to Tuscaloosa. They traveled by covered wagons, bringing their handsome mahogany furniture and other family heirlooms. Some of this furniture stood proudly in the Drish home. But that was later.

In Tuscaloosa, Mrs. McKinney met and married Dr. John Drish, a physician whose wife had died some time before. Dr. Drish had one child, Katherine, a beautiful young lady who, heartbroken by a love affair which her father's stern intervention had terminated and further tormented by a miserable marriage, had lost her mind.

About 1830 Dr. and Mrs. Drish built on the outskirts of Tuscaloosa (now in the residential-business section on 17th Street between Greensboro and Queen City avenues)

About 1830 Dr. and Mrs. Drish built an imposing plantation home.

an imposing plantation home.

The house can probably best be described as Southern colonial with strong Greek and Italian Renaissance influence. A wide porch with stark Doric columns extends across the rear, and the front is distinguished by two Ionic columns on each side of a large square tower rising from the middle of the porch. The main entrance to the home is through the arched door on the ground level of the three-story tower.

Above the entrance is a square room which opens into an upstairs hall. A winding stairway leads from this room to the square tower room which stands above the level of the flat roof.

At the rear of the large downstairs hall a horseshoe staircase rises in a graceful curve to the landing where straight flights, one on each side, ascend to the upstairs hall.

Mrs. Drish was evidently a woman of excellent taste and of impressive financial means. Rich velvet carpets covered the floors of her home, imported lace curtains hung at the windows, and the soft glow of candles danced in the crystal prisms of the candelabra on the marble mantel.

A lodge at the main entrance to the estate provided shelter for the slaves whose duty it was to open and close the heavy gates. A long driveway bordered by flowering shrubs and evergreens led from the gate to the house. One approach was bordered with pink and white altheas, and in the formal gardens were thousands of roses. Beyond the gardens were the fruit orchards, and beyond them stretched the fields and woods.

Such an elaborate estate required much attention. Dr. Drish was unfortunately a very poor manager. It was widely reported that he "gambled and drank—and did both very poorly." Often, the story goes, he would take a boatload of cotton from his plantation down the river to

Mobile to sell. Weeks later he would return to Tuscaloosa with nothing except a terrific hangover and a remorseful conscience. Usually he had to be put to bed and carefully nursed for some time.

It was after one such trip that, tormented by his own guilt and by sadness over Katherine's increasing madness, he broke from the restraining arms of servants trying to hold him on the bed, stumbled to the curved stairway, shrieked, and died.

For many years after his death Negroes on the plantation often claimed they heard Dr. Drish's stumbling footsteps followed by his agonized cry.

Before his burial, Dr. Drish's body lay in state with candles burning around the bier, the same candles that were to provide another restless spirit with a reason for haunting the Drish house.

Mrs. Drish, after the funeral, asked that these candles be put away to be saved until her death when they were to be lighted again around her coffin.

Following Dr. Drish's death Mrs. Drish's niece, Mrs. Virginia Owen Green, her husband, Thomas Finley Green, and their children came to live with her. The happy confusion of having children in the house was a delight, particularly to Katherine who had become more and more silent and withdrawn.

Through the years Mrs. Drish maintained an alert interest in the happenings beyond her dwindling estate. Records show that, despite her old age and loss of wealth, she continued to subscribe to and read *The Philadelphia Times, The New Orleans Picayune, Godey's Ladies' Book, The London Illustrated News, Littel's Living Age, Appleton's Journal*, and other periodicals. And she insisted that the accustomed ceremonies of gracious living which had been practiced in less poverty-stricken years be continued as far as was possible. As she grew older she was particularly concerned that the death rites she desired be observed, especially that the same candles which had burned after Dr. Drish's death light her coffin while she lay in state.

When Mrs. Drish died one of the old servants reminded Mrs. Green of the dead woman's almost obsessive wish.

"Ole Miss said a hundred times she want them same candles burned," the servant prompted Mrs. Green.

The niece made a search, not a very diligent one, for the candles, but they were not found. Mrs. Green had not been present for Dr. Drish's funeral and did not attach any real significance to her aunt's request concerning the candles, possibly dismissing it as a whim of an old and addled woman.

She paid no heed, except for a show of impatience, when the servant kept repeating, "We got to find them candles. Ole Miss going to walk if we don't find them candles and burn them like she say. Ole Miss sure gonna walk!"

The candles were not found, and Mrs. Drish, though given a proper funeral, was buried without their having been burned.

Soon afterwards began the strange appearances of fire in the tower room, sightings which for many years caused the occupants of the house to be ousted from their beds by false fire alarms.

Some people tried to find scientific explanations for the fiery lights in the tower, but those wise in the ways of the spirit world never doubted that "Ole Miss" was indeed walking and had come back to her home to burn her own death candles.

Most Alabama homes are content to provide habitation for only one ghost, but the Drish house has had several ghostly inhabitants. Not only have both Dr. Drish and Mrs. Drish returned, but another and in some respects even stranger presence has manifested itself there.

After the death of Mrs. Drish, Mr. and Mrs. Green closed the upstairs of the house and converted the two downstairs parlors into bedrooms. Katherine had been sent, before Mrs. Drish's death, to be cared for by family members in another state, and so there were not enough people living in the house to necessitate the use of the upstairs portion.

Mary, fourteen years old, and her sister, Nimmo, a year younger, slept in the front parlor, and their parents shared the bedroom in the converted back parlor. The folding doors between the two rooms were kept locked.

One night Mary and Nimmo had been invited to a spend-the-night party at their cousins' home, but Nimmo had a headache and stayed at home, going to bed alone in the front bedroom.

Her headache kept Nimmo from sleeping, but, when she heard the hall door open softly, she pretended to be asleep so that her mother would not worry about her. She lay quite still and kept her eyes closed while gentle hands straightened the covers and tucked them snugly around her. Not until the soft sound of the tiptoes had died away and she heard the latch on the hall door click did Nimmo open her eyes. She laughed to herself at the joke she had played on her mother.

The next morning at breakfast she confessed, "Mother, I was just pretending to be asleep when you came into my room and covered me up last night."

Her mother was amazed. "I didn't come to your room, dear," she said. "You must have had a vivid dream."

However, she and her mother agreed not to mention the episode to Mary as they did not want to frighten her.

29

The next night the sisters were in their big bed, and Nimmo was sleeping soundly when Mary clutched her and sobbed in fright.

"Nimmo! Nimmo, wake up!! Somebody came in here and covered us up. I thought at first it was Mother, but it wasn't. Whoever it was wouldn't answer me, wouldn't say anything at all!"

The child was almost hysterical, and Nimmo was frightened too, but she calmed her sister enough so that they could go together to their parents' room.

They waked their father and mother, both of whom had been sound asleep, and told them what had happened. With Mr. Green leading the way, they made a thorough search of the house, but every door and every window was locked. Nobody was there.

Some forty years later, when Mary and Nimmo were middle-aged women, they were spending a vacation at Alabama's White Sulphur Springs, a popular resort in De-Kalb County.

One night the guests were gathered on the wide veranda entertaining each other by telling of unusual or weird things that had happened to them.

Mrs. G. W. Cochrane of Mobile announced to the group that she knew a ghost story more exciting than any that had been told.

Her sister, Mrs. Cochrane said, had come to Tuscaloosa to visit her while she and Judge Cochrane were living in an old home there. The sister, young and popular, was invited to a number of parties at the University of Alabama, among them the Commencement Ball.

On the night of the ball she complained of a slight headache, perhaps brought on by lack of sleep, but she got dressed for the festivity, and, while waiting for her escort, she decided to lie down to rest for a few minutes.

30

As she lay in the darkened room, the door opened lightly, someone tiptoed across the room, and tender hands pulled up a coverlet and tucked it about her.

The guest turned to thank her sister—but there was no one there!

Screams brought Judge and Mrs. Cochrane to the room immediately. They searched the house, but no trace of an intruder could be found.

When Mrs. Cochrane finished her story, Mary and Nimmo exchanged glances. Then, to the amazement of the audience, they named the house and the very room where the incident had occurred: the downstairs front parlor in the old Drish Place.

The Drish home is now part of the educational building of the Southside Baptist Church in Tuscaloosa. This latest change in ownership should have exorcised the ghosts. But on some nights there still appear to be lights in the tower room, the kind of lights cast by flickering candles.

31

Here in the tower, with its triple windows on all four sides, Anne and her play-mates spent many happy hours.

Carlisle Hall looks almost exactly today as it did when completed in 1837.

The Faithful Vigil at Carlisle Hall

ARLISLE HALL DOES NOT conform to the accepted notion of a Southern plantation home: it has no white columns, no broad verandas, no delicate iron grillwork trim. Instead it is a solid, sensible structure made of brick and trimmed in pale pink fieldstone. Its doors and windows are arched, and its plain balcony with the copper-roofed overhang is more Oriental than Grecian.

There is little in the appearance of Carlisle Hall to suggest that it has a ghost, yet there is somehow a vague atmosphere of gloomy foreboding about the place.

Except for its front porch, which has been altered from its original proportions, Carlisle Hall looks almost exactly as it did when it was completed in 1837.

Edwin Kenworthy Carlisle chose for the site of his home a hilltop covered with oaks and hardwoods, some of which still shade the house today. Ten years in the building, the dwelling is a short distance off the main highway about a mile west of Marion in Perry County.

The brick and the sandstone used in building Carlisle Hall were imported from Europe, probably coming over as ballast in ships docking in Mobile. Thousands and thousands of bricks were used to build the eighteen-room house with its twenty-eight-inch-thick walls. Carlisle did not skimp on the bricks nor on the fine oak woodwork used in the doors, the stairways, and the wainscoting. Even the mortar was the finest available and is still in perfect condition today.

It was in this massive house that Anne Carlisle was born, that she grew up to young womanhood, and that she died. And it is here that her weeping ghost still wanders.

Anne had a carefree childhood, building playhouses under the shady oaks; sitting on the steps of the brick kitchen, which was separated from the house by a short walkway, to listen to songs and stories composed for her pleasure by the cook and the yardman; dressing up in frills and ruffles to pass the napkins when her mother served tea to afternoon callers; riding her pony with her father to watch the slaves work in the fields; or, perhaps best of all, climbing the spiral staircase up to the square tower room that dominates Carlisle Hall. Here in the tower, with its triple windows on all four sides, Anne and her play-mates spent many happy hours.

The tower was Anne's favorite room at Carlisle Hall.

As she grew older, she loved to go up to the tower to be alone. She would sit for hours on the broad window ledge, gazing out across the countryside and dreaming romantic dreams of the future.

In those dreams was a young man, a neighbor. As children they had played together around Carlisle Hall's spacious ground and in the tower room, and they had laughingly talked of marriage "when we get big." Now they were "big"—grown up—and again they talked of marriage. It was not a game this time though, not a bit of playtime fantasy to laugh about. The Civil War had begun. Their plans for marriage were tinged with uncertainty and sadness, and sometimes Anne wondered if they would ever again share such carefree laughter as they had known in childhood.

Anne's lover had been among the first from Perry County to volunteer for service in the Confederate Army. Although he and Anne were deeply in love, they felt they could not marry until the war had ended. They had discussed plans for their future again and again, and always the young man said, "Don't worry, Anne. The war won't last long. I'll soon be back home, and we can have the wonderful wedding we used to talk about when we were children playing in the tower room. Remember? You just wait for me."

And Anne promised to wait.

Before he rode off to join the Confederate forces, the gray-clad youth paid a final visit to Carlisle Hall to say good-bye to Anne. As was frequently done by affluent young Southerners going off to war, Anne's lover took his personal servant with him, a slave named Big Tom. Big Tom waited at the curving approach to Carlisle Hall that day while his master talked to Anne and told her good-bye.

During that final conversation the couple agreed that Big Tom would return to Carlisle Hall to bring news of his master after the first battle ended. Anne believed with a nearly fanatic obsession that if her lover was not harmed during his first battle, he would be spared to return to her when the war was over. He, being a realistic man, probably did not share Anne's belief, but he humored her by agreeing to the plan.

"If you are all right, let Big Tom come riding back

Over his head fluttered a dark red flag.

waving a white flag. If you have been killed—God forbid —let him carry a red flag. I'll be watching from the tower window," Anne told her lover.

And so began Anne's weeks of vigil. Each morning she climbed the narrow stairs to the tower room where she sat on the window ledge hour after hour, looking across the treetops to the road that leads up the hill to Carlisle Hall. Her maid brought her meals up to her, and members of her family joined her frequently to talk with her and thus help pass the time, but so intent was Anne on watching for Big Tom to arrive with his message that she was scarcely aware of the food or of the companionship. Only when it grew too dark to see the road would she come down from the tower room.

One day at noon while Anne was eating her solitary meal she heard the sound of a horse approaching Carlisle Hall at a full gallop. She threw her tray to the floor and hurried to the window. She knew with a strange certainty that the horseman was Big Tom bringing her a message.

Now after weeks of waiting Anne was filled with a sense of dread and foreboding so great that only by exerting the strongest willpower could she force herself to look out at the clearing where the rider would first come into sight. As she made herself look, Big Tom rode into the clearing.

Over his head fluttered a dark red flag.

For a moment Anne stood hypnotized, unable to take her eyes off the approaching red flag. Then, calling her dead lover's name, she flung herself over the stair rail and fell down through the spiral stairwell to the hall three floors below.

When her father, who had heard her scream, reached her, Anne was dead.

Many families have occupied Carlisle Hall since Anne's

tragic death, and for long periods of time it has stood empty. Yet even now, after more than one hundred years, the cries of Anne Carlisle can still be heard as she goes to join her lover in death.

The Specter in the Maze at Cahaba

NTEBELLUM CAHABA WAS A pleasant place to live.

There seemed to be no limit to the round of entertainment and visiting in the Dallas County town. Fine carriages awaited the arrival of each boat at the Cahaba landing to convey passengers to the homes where they would be guests.

Down Vine Street, Cahaba's principal business section, they drove, past its paved walks shaded by ancient water oaks, mulberry and chinaberry trees, past the newspaper offices, the churches, the stores, the telegraph office.

Just outside of town was the racetrack. Sometimes the rider who won the race would receive a silver-trimmed saddle as a prize, but some of the spectators won far more valuable monetary trophies.

Beyond the racetrack was a secluded spot where cock fighting and, occasionally, gander pullings attracted the younger gentlemen of the neighborhood. These sports, however, were frowned upon by their elders, and those who frequented them never talked about these events at home.

If the guests drove through Cahaba in the afternoon, they would likely see the town's lawyers and doctors sitting along the shady sidewalks with their chairs tilted back and their feet resting on the gnarled tree trunks, laughing and talking until lengthened shadows signaled time for supper.

There was Saltmarsh Hall, scene of masked balls, enactments of romantic scenes from Byron and Moore, fanciful tableau, and political orations fiery with talk of secession.

Here at Saltmarsh Hall the battle flag was presented to the Cahaba Rifles before the unit departed for service in the Confederate Army. The flag, which was in front on every field of battle from Manassas to Fredericksburg, was accepted by Colonel C. C. Pegues (then a captain), commanding officer of the Cahaba Rifles, Company F, Fifth Alabama Regiment.

It was this Confederate officer, Colonel Pegues, who owned the property at which the ghostly phenomenon bearing his name manifested itself.

There were grander and costlier homes in Cahaba than the one occupied by Colonel Pegues and his family, but none could surpass it in hospitality.

The house had been a jail during the years 1820-1826 when Cahaba was the capital of Alabama, a background that provided the Pegues family much amusement. After Colonel Pegues purchased the property, he planned and supervised its renovation so expertly that it bore no resemblance to the place of incarceration it had once been.

The Pegues home fronted on Pine Street and occupied the entire block between Pine and Chestnut. Magnolia trees, Lombardy pines, and oaks grew about the grounds, and flower gardens and fountains added to the tranquil beauty of the place.

The most distinctive feature of the premises, and the one most enjoyed by young guests, was the labyrinth or maze of thick cedars. No place in Cahaba was more popular with couples out for a stroll than was this evergreen labyrinth, and leisurely walks through the Pegues' maze became a part of the ritual of courtship in Cahaba.

So it was that one soft moonlight night in the spring of 1862 a young Confederate soldier and his sweetheart were promenading in the Pegues' garden. He had only a few days leave, and there was much he wanted to say to the beautiful girl beside him.

Before the promenade began the young people had paid a proper call on the elders in the Pegues' home. The soldier, perhaps, had brought messages from Colonel Pegues who was then in Virginia with the Cahaba Rifles.

This duty discharged, they now turned their thoughts from the tragedy of war to the joy of their own reunion.

Their stroll led them naturally to the maze of cedars. They had entered one of the circular walks leading to the center of the labyrinth when a large, white glowing ball darted toward them. It appeared to be floating in the air a few feet above the ground as though controlled by some powerful but invisible force.

The ball played a taunting game with them, swerving from one side of the walk to the other, and then hovering directly in front of the couple, almost daring them to catch it. Then it would recede and disappear in the thick cedars, reappearing seconds later right beside the startled pair.

The soldier, being accustomed to having solid and logical explanations for all happenings, was at a loss to explain the antics of the luminous ball or to account for its origin, but he decided that it was an illusion caused by the reflections of the moonlight on some object hidden

41

from their view.

"Don't be frightened," he said, putting his arm gently and protectively around the girl's waist. "It's just some trick the moonlight is playing. Let's walk back toward the house—I'm sure the thing won't appear again."

But it did.

They had retraced their steps only a short distance through the maze when the bright sphere appeared in front of them and began performing all sorts of gyrations. This time, motivated by both curiosity and exasperation, the soldier jumped toward the object and tried to catch it, but just as he seemed to have it in his grasp, the ball twirled away and disappeared completely.

When the young people returned to the Pegues' house with their strange story, they were accused of being "moonstruck." However, the account of their encounter with the apparition was upsetting to the women of the household who wished, more fervently than ever, that Colonel Pegues were at home to protect them from whatever it was that was cavorting around in the night.

After its initial appearance the dancing ball of light was seen by several other persons. Their stories of its erratic behavior differed only in small details from the accounts given by the couple who first saw it.

The phenomenon became known as "Pegues' Ghost," and stories of its antics were told throughout the countryside. Strolling in the maze became more popular than ever as couples hoped—yet feared—that they might also have an encounter with the eerie object. And what girl could object to having a strong, protective arm around her in such frightening surroundings?

Colonel Pegues himself probably never heard about the ghostly ball which bears his name. He was mortally wounded in the battle of Gaines' Mill, Virginia, on June

This time the soldier jumped toward the object and tried to catch it.

27, 1862, and died July 15, 1862. He was buried at Hollywood Cemetery in Richmond, Virginia.

When news of his death reached Cahaba, a Negro boy ringing a bell went from house to house carrying a black-bordered funeral notice. From the messenger's shoulders flowed long black streamers known as "weepers," a Cahaba custom which has long since disappeared.

Gone, too, are the old Pegues home, the flowering shrubs, the fountains, and the maze. A few clumps of old-fashioned yellow jonquils and some scattered piles of broken brick are all that remain to mark the scene where the strangely bright Pegues' Ghost caused such excitement more than a century ago.

A few clumps of old-fashioned yellow jonquills mark the scene where Pegues'
ghost caused such excitement more than a century ago.

A hunter trying to follow the baying of his hound will report seeing a white fireball.

But stories of the glowing ball are still told, and, occasionally, a fisherman returning home late at night from an outing on the river or a hunter trying to follow the baying of his hound will report seeing a white fireball near where the circles of cedars once provided background for a supernatural display.

Superstitious rivermen who see the ghostly hull rise from the water leave the river for safer jobs ashore.

The Phantom Steamboat of the Tombigbee

HEN THE LATE WINTER rains send the Tombigbee River out of its banks at Nanafalia, Tuscahoma, Naheola, and Yellow Bluff, there sometimes rises out of the muddy water a ghost ship, the charred hull of a sidewheel steamer.

On those stormy nights some folks along the river say they hear the gay music of a steam calliope, and others report hearing agonizing cries for help blown on the cold river wind.

"It's the *Eliza Battle*," whisper the folks who see the phantom boat and who hear the eerie sounds. "It's the *Eliza Battle* trying to finish her trip down to Mobile. Something terrible is going to happen!"

For always the appearance of the phantom ship has heralded tragedy. Superstitious rivermen who see the ghostly hull rise from the water leave the river for safer jobs ashore: they know that the *Eliza Battle* is warning them that the treacherous Tombigbee will claim their lives just as it claimed the lives of passengers and crew on the *Eliza Battle*.

The *Eliza Battle* was one of the grandest steamers on the Tombigbee. Built in New Albany, Indiana, in 1852, she was a palatial boat, and her trips up and down the Tombigbee created excitement wherever she stopped. And no trip was so fine or so grand as her last, the one that began in late February, 1858.

The *Eliza Battle's* trip down to Mobile had been advertised for weeks with circulars, handbills and newspaper ads. In addition to the customary luxuries, the passengers were promised two bands to provide continuous music in the ballroom, glowing lanterns to decorate the entire ship at night, colorful flags and bunting draped and festooned on every deck, a calliope to play the latest tunes, and welcoming celebrations at landings all along the way.

So an eager and carefree crowd of passengers was attracted aboard the *Eliza Battle*, bound for Mobile and the gaiety of that port city.

At Columbus they began to assemble. Ladies wearing full skirts, so fashionable then, and carrying tiny parasols chatted excitedly as they boarded the boat. Behind them came their personal maids, and behind the maids came burly porters carrying trunks and valises and hatboxes.

On the wharf the men, plantation owners all, supervised the loading of their bales of cotton. Taking the cotton down to Mobile to sell provided their excuse for the trip.

Carriages came from plantations throughout the area, and each group of new arrivals sparked fresh merriment as friends and relatives who had not seen each other in many months were reunited aboard the *Eliza Battle*.

When the last bale of cotton had been loaded and the last valise had been put into the staterooms (some observers feared the cargo was too heavy), the band struck up a lively tune, the deep-voiced whistles sounded, and the crowd cheered as the *Eliza Battle* pulled away from the wharf and headed downstream.

The scene was repeated on a smaller scale at landing after landing as, up in the pilot house, Daniel Eppes guided the *Eliza Battle* down the river toward Mobile.

Crowds of people bundled in wraps as protection against the increasing cold waited along the banks of the river to cheer and wave as the *Eliza Battle* passed, and their salutes were acknowledged by shrill trills from the calliope. After nightfall some spectators set off rockets and other fireworks as the *Eliza Battle* went steaming past.

Eppes, a veteran pilot, was uneasy. The high water had covered many of his navigation points, and the heavily-loaded vessel was difficult to handle in the swift current. The strong and bitterly cold wind blowing rain in from the northwest added to his apprehension. Then, about nightfall, the rain turned to sleet mixed with snow as the temperature continued to drop rapidly.

Capt. S. G. Stone, master of the *Eliza Battle*, joined Eppes in the pilot house, and together they peered through the storm for familiar lights and landmarks. The sandbars and the shoals were covered by the swirling waters, and even the tall trees along the banks of the river were half submerged. The river seemed to stretch endlessly in all directions. Eppes relied on his knowledge and experience to keep the *Eliza Battle* in the main channel.

He checked Mrs. Kemp's landing on his chart as the boat moved past that point, and he breathed a prayer of gratitude for safe passage that far. But he became increasingly anxious.

The uneasiness of the pilot and the concern of the captain were not shared by the passengers. The brilliant

49

Passengers jumped into the water as they tried to escape the advancing flames.

lights in the ballroom pushed back all awareness of the menacing darkness outside, and the music of the bands drowned out the noise of the slashing storm. Long after midnight the dancing continued as the partners whirled and glided on the polished floor.

Then above the music and the laughter came the cries of, "Fire! Fire!"

The music, the laughter, and the dancing stopped.

Men and women rushed for the exits. Even before they reached the deck, flames were leaping from blazing cotton bales and racing through the engine room, the cabins, the gangways.

Captain Stone ordered the pilot to run the boat into the riverbank, but the tiller rope had been burned and Eppes could not carry out the order. The *Eliza Battle*, ablaze from bow to stern, drifted crazily with the current.

Passengers jumped into the icy water as they tried to escape the advancing flames. Some of them threw bales of cotton off the deck and attempted to use them for life rafts. Those who could swim fought the current to find temporary safety in the tops of the nearly-submerged trees where they clung to limbs and prayed to be rescued before they froze.

For a little while the flames from the burning boat lighted the scene, but soon the blazing hull drifted downstream, and the darkness and bitter cold closed in on the survivors.

From the darkness came pitiful cries for help and prayers for deliverance. There were other sounds, too: the heavy splashes of frozen bodies dropping into the river from the trees.

The tragedy produced its heroes. Among them was Frank Stone, second clerk of the boat, who swam ashore carrying to safety a child of Mr. and Mrs. Bat Cromwell

51

of Mobile. He then placed a Miss Turner on a bale of cotton and guided her to the riverbank. His efforts to save her sister and her mother failed: the sister froze to death in his arms, and the mother died of cold while clinging to a tree.

The glare from the burning boat and the screams of the victims aroused the inhabitants of Naheola, a landing some thirty miles below Demopolis, and they hurried to the river to give what help they could.

Soon the blazing hull of the Eliza Battle drifted downstream and sank here in the Tombigbee.

In the group was James Eskridge who commandeered a skiff, the only one available, and paddled through the freezing storm to rescue survivors from treetops, from floating cotton bales, and from the edge of the water. For hour after endless hour he maneuvered the small boat through the dark water looking for survivors. Some witnesses credited him with bringing as many as one hundred persons to safety.

Meanwhile, as news of the tragedy spread, planters from nearby plantations arrived with their skilled workmen who hastily built rafts and joined in the rescue operation. Later these carpenters made rough coffins for the dead.

People on the bank lighted huge bonfires to provide illumination for the rescuers and warmth for the nearly-frozen survivors.

As they were saved from the river, the passengers were taken to the large home of Mrs. Rebecca Coleman Pettigrew where the house itself and all the outbuildings were converted into makeshift hospitals for the care of the injured and ill. At one time seventy-five persons were being cared for by Mrs. Pettigrew, her family, and her servants.

All of her teams and wagons were assigned to hauling wood for the roaring fires which kept the cold from claiming additional victims. Huge cauldrons of soup bubbled day and night to provide food for the survivors. For almost a week Mrs. Pettigrew gave her full time to the care of her guests, doing everything possible for their comfort until their families could come for them.

When the weather finally cleared and the river began to recede, the mournful task of recovering the bodies of the dead was completed. Nobody now knows exactly how many lives were lost in the disaster. Some say twenty-nine, some say more than fifty, but they all agree that the burning of the *Eliza Battle* was probably the greatest tragedy in Alabama's river history.

For years afterwards people who lived close to the river, who loved her and understood her moods, said the ghost of the *Eliza Battle* still plied the 'Bigbee's waters. On stormy nights, they said, they saw the great steamer rise up out of the troubled water. The boat, they said, was ablaze from bow to stern, so brightly lighted that the name *Eliza Battle* could be read plainly on even the darkest nights.

And always there was music, dancing tunes, providing a background for the shrieks of terror and cries for help that came from the phantom vessel.

Tales about the ghost vessel became a part of traditional Tombigbee River lore.

Most often these apparitions were seen by crewmen of tugs and barges, and when these rivermen reached Mobile they usually began looking for jobs ashore, safer employment away from the threatening river.

Sometimes, speaking cautiously, they would describe the ghost ship to friends along the waterfront. And their listeners, rivermen like themselves, would nod with understanding.

They had seen the *Eliza Battle*, too.

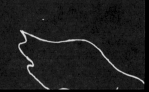

The Unquiet Ghost at Gaineswood

T IS AN ACCEPTED AXIOM which has persisted from the time of Homer to this day that no ghost can rest quietly until his body has been given proper burial. Those unfortunates who have not been interred with the necessary rites are doomed to haunt the earth until their remains are put into their graves with due ceremony. Gaineswood, the great house built in Demopolis by General Nathan B. Whitfield in 1842, has been haunted by such a restless ghost.

General Whitfield began the building of his home in 1842, and when it was completed it was the showplace of Alabama. His friend, George Strother Gaines, the Choctaw Indian factor, had lived on the site, and General Whitfield decided that it was most fitting for the mansion to be named for him.

No ghost could have found a more beautiful house to haunt than this neoclassic mansion with its twelve great Doric columns on the portico, in pleasing contrast with the more elaborate Corinthian drawing room and the priceless Chippendale furniture throughout the house.

Soon after Gaineswood was completed Mrs. Whitfield died, leaving several small children, and the general found it necessary to employ a housekeeper. He was fortunate enough to find an efficient and attractive young woman, a Miss Carter, whose father was in Europe serving as consul to Greece at the time.

General Whitfield built this great house in Demopolis and called it

Miss Carter's relatives lived in Virginia, far away from the Marengo County town of Demopolis, and despite her duties as housekeeper for the large mansion and as companion for the children she was often lonely. General Whitfield was aware of her loneliness, so, being a kind and thoughtful man, he was pleased for her to invite her sister Evelyn to come to Gaineswood to spend the winter with her.

Evelyn was an excellent musician and loved to play

Gaineswood. No ghost could have found a more beautiful house to haunt.

Together they created stirring, rousing music that filled the spacious rooms of Gaineswood.

the piano. The General was also an accomplished musician, and he encouraged Evelyn to perform. He particularly liked for her to play the martial tunes of Scotland, and on occasion he would bring out his bagpipes to play duets. Together they created stirring, rousing music that filled the spacious rooms of Gaineswood and spilled over into the countryside.

Evelyn's presence at Gaineswood brought happiness and cheer to the entire family. In spite of a winter of severe weather, the coldest Alabama had experienced in many, many years, life at Gaineswood was pleasant until Evelyn became sick. Although General Whitfield provided the best medical care available, after several weeks of illness she died.

Nobody remembers exactly what it was that brought about her death. Some say she had a severe attack of malaria, others contend that it was pneumonia, and it has been rumored that she pined away because of a disappointment in love.

There was a handsome young French count (he had come to Demopolis to visit his relatives among the Napoleonic exiles who settled there) who often visited Gaineswood. He appeared to be quite interested in Evelyn. It is said that he even bought an engagement ring for her, but they quarreled and he snatched the ring, hurled it into the shrubbery, and left, never to return. Evelyn's decline was attributed to the grief following this unfortunate love affair.

Whatever the cause, Evelyn died.

Because the roads were covered with ice and snow, it was impossible to have her body carried to Virginia as she had requested. Besides, it would take time for her father to return from Greece, and one of her final wishes was that he be present for her funeral. It was decided, therefore, that her burial should be postponed until spring so that her last wishes could be fulfilled.

In those days there were no embalmers anywhere near Gaineswood. To preserve her body, Evelyn's casket was placed in a heavy pine box which was sealed airtight with rosin.

This box was stored under the stairs in the cellar until good weather and the return of Evelyn's father would make it possible to have a proper funeral in her own family's Virginia burying ground.

She did not like being sealed in that box and kept in the cold, dark cellar.

As is true of all ghosts, the one thing Evelyn wanted most was to be buried so that she could rest peacefully in her own grave. She did not like being sealed in that box and kept in the cold, dark cellar.

Soon after her death the people in the house began hearing footsteps coming up the stairs from the cellar. Then they would hear the sound of tiptoes going into the drawing room where the big square piano stood. After that, faint sounds of music would float out into the hall and up the stairs to the bedrooms. Many of the tunes were those of the staunch Scottish ballads that Evelyn used to play, but the plaintive, homesick melodies of Stephen Foster were heard too. These mournful sounds distressed the listeners for they reminded them that Evelyn was unhappy.

On the occasions when the braver members of the household would creep downstairs to investigate the source of the disturbing sounds the music would stop abruptly, but as soon as they returned upstairs the sad melodies would begin again.

Those recurrent footsteps and the eerie music so interrupted the sleep of the family that they were greatly relieved when the weather moderated and Evelyn's body could be taken to Virginia for burial.

But if the family at Gaineswood thought Evelyn's burial in Virginia would bring a complete halt to the night-time visitations, they were mistaken.

Evidently Evelyn could not forgive them for keeping her so long under the stairs in the cellar. While her midnight wanderings were not so frequent as they had been, she did continue to return to Gaineswood occasionally.

People who have spent the night at Gaineswood in recent years insist that their dreams have been interrupted by the sound of soft footsteps on the cellar stairs and by the lilting, tinkling melodies of half-forgotten songs of long ago. And they are sure that the ghost of Evelyn Carter returns to protest her exile in the sealed pine box beneath the cellar stairs at Gaineswood.

Carrollton Courthouse
in
Pickens County

It is still there, plainly visible
on the lower right-hand pane
of the garret window.

The Face in the Courthouse Window

SINCE 1878 THERE HAS BEEN the picture of a man's face so indelibly stamped on a window of the Pickens County Courthouse that it looks as if a photographer had snapped his lens and made the likeness on the glass pane.

But it was no human photographer who reproduced that countenance, which reflects the anguish and terror filling the heart of a man who knew that he was face to face with violent death.

The courthouse in Carrollton was burned to the ground on Thursday morning, November 16, 1876. Fire broke out in several places at the same time, and for this reason the blaze was held unquestionably to be the work of an incendiary.

The burning of the courthouse unleashed an emotional torrent that swept away both patience and reason. The courthouse was more to the residents than just a seat of county government: it was a symbol of their defiance of

Yankee authority, sturdy evidence of their determination to overcome defeat.

The original courthouse had been burned by Yankee troops under the Command of General John T. Croxton on April 5, 1865. It was a senseless burning, serving no military purpose, and it infuriated and embittered the residents of the county.

In those days following the Civil War the task of rebuilding the courthouse seemed impossible. There was no money. Materials were scarce and expensive. Skilled labor was difficult to find. Yet somehow the courthouse was rebuilt. Even the occupying Federal troops who were camped in Carrollton during the postwar years must have been impressed by the achievement.

To the citizens whose work and sacrifice had rebuilt the courthouse the building represented a restoration of law and order: it was important to their sense of stability as well as to their pride.

Then, less than twelve years after their first courthouse was burned by the Yankees, the residents of Carrollton watched helplessly as their second courthouse, the one they had struggled so hard to rebuild, was consumed by fire. It was almost more than they could bear.

As time went on and nobody was able to point the finger of justice at any suspect, the citizens of Carrollton became uneasy and began to criticize the officers of the law for not finding the criminal. They demanded that the sheriff produce the person who had burned the courthouse so that they could sleep easy in their beds at night without waking frequently to see if they smelled something burning. The sheriff realized that he must find a suspect if he possibly could.

Henry Wells, a Negro who lived near the town, had a bad name. His temper was high and he had been involved in several fights. It was rumored that he always carried a razor.

Nobody really saw him set fire to the courthouse, but he had been in town early on the morning when the fire occurred, and rumors connecting him with the burning began to be circulated—especially when no other suspect could be located.

In spite of the fact that there was only vague circumstantial evidence against him, Wells was arrested on four counts: arson, burglary, carrying a concealed weapon, and assault with intent to murder.

Wells swore that he was not guilty and was being wrongly accused, but in a group of men gathered about the square on the sultry afternoon of his arrest feeling against him ran high, and with the aid of some corn whiskey it ran higher until it reached a dangerous pitch.

The air on that afternoon was oppressively humid. In a black ragged cloud west of town the rumbling of thunder lent an additional menace to the already ominous situation. Men began milling about, demanding immediate action against Wells. Soon someone produced a rope, and hasty plans for hanging him at once were made.

In an effort to save him from the excited crowd the sheriff hid Wells in the garret of the new courthouse, but his whereabouts were soon discovered and bent on vengeance the angry horde closed in on the courthouse, ready to break down its doors if necessary to reach their prey.

Wells knew why they were there, but he went to the garret window, his face grey with fear, and confronted them, defiantly shouting at the top of his lungs, "I am innocent. If you kill me, I am going to haunt you for the rest of your lives!" And as later events proved, he did.

Just as the bloodthirsty crowd was about to get into the building a bolt of lightning illuminated Wells' tortured face behind the windowpane. The hot, close atmosphere of the afternoon had been the prelude to a short but severe thunderstorm, and Henry Wells' picture caught by the lightning, they say, has remained imprinted on the garret window of the Carrollton courthouse from that day to this.

Accounts vary as to how Wells actually met his death. As one story has it, the lightning killed him. Then, sobered by this event, the crowd dispersed, satisfied that the Almighty had meted out just punishment to a criminal.

Another version of the tale is that the lightning flash alarmed the mob, but not enough to stop them from hanging their victim. At any rate, everyone agrees that this was the last night of Henry Wells' life.

The next morning, a calm day after the tumultuous night, a member of the lynching party was passing the courthouse. He glanced up at the window where he had seen Wells looking out the night before, and he turned pale with fright. He rubbed his eyes, and, silently cursing the corn whiskey he had drunk the night before, he looked again—and again he saw the face of Henry Wells peering down at him. He knew that Wells was dead, and he began to scream that the devil had come to haunt him.

His screams brought other people to the scene, and they, too, saw the face of Henry Wells, distorted by fear but an unmistakable likeness, looking down at them.

"I am innocent. If you kill me, I am going to haunt you for the rest of your lives!"

*His screams brought other people to the scene, where the face of Henry Wells,
distorted by fear but an unmistakable likeness, looked down at them.*

The face was still there the next day, and the next, and the next. Hundreds of people came to gaze in awe and disbelief at the eerie likeness.

The sheriff was particularly upset by the accusing face. He was often seen carrying buckets of water up the steep stairs to try to wash away the symbol of a town's guilt, but he only succeeded in making the picture more clearly defined. No amount of scrubbing, not even with gasoline, would remove the image from the windowpane.

It is still there, plainly visible on the lower right-hand pane of the garret window. On at least one occasion, some people say two, every windowpane in the Carrollton courthouse was broken during a severe hailstorm—except the pane with the image of Henry Wells on it.

And on stormy nights, some people swear they can hear Wells' wails coming from the twisted mouth of the face in the window.

Often he stopped to rest on a bench beneath the giant oaks in Bienville Square not far from his Mobile home.

Mobile's Pipe-Smoking Sea Captain

HE CAPTAIN HAD THE ROLL-
ing gait of a man who had done
most of his walking on the decks
of ships and who had sailed long
enough to set his pulses throbbing
with the rhythm of the sea.

No one now living remembers him, but many people
recall hearing their grandparents tell about this strange
man, so silent and withdrawn that his neighbors on Mobile's
State Street had hardly more than a nodding acquaintance
with him.

These neighbors called him simply the Captain, and
after awhile it seemed that he had no other name. It was
rumored that he had left his ship after an angry disagreement with another officer, and the Captain had stubbornly
refused to apologize for his hasty, bitter words.

After he moved into the house on State Street, he
was often seen pacing restlessly about in his yard. On fair
days and foul he wore his captain's cap set firmly on his
greying hair, and, as he paced, he blew clouds of smoke

from his stubby pipe. So constantly did he smoke his pipe, it seemed almost a physical part of him.

Some people said that the Captain had seen every great seaport in the world and that his house was filled with curios collected in faraway places. Few people ever saw these treasures, though, for the Captain almost never had guests.

For awhile after he moved to State Street, seafaring friends in town between voyages used to come to see him, but gradually their visits became more and more infrequent and they finally ceased entirely.

The Captain was obviously lonely, but he rejected all gestures of friendship from his neighbors. He could not be congenial with landlubbers who had never known the wonder and majesty of the sea; he yearned for companions who shared his love for ships and whitecaps and churning waters.

Sometimes his homesickness for ships and water exerted a pull as strong as the tide itself, and he would spend entire days along the docks watching freighters load and unload their cargoes. These were his happiest times. Late in the afternoon, after a day along the waterfront, he would give a smart salute to a ship moving out of the harbor, and then he would turn toward home, never looking back. Often he stopped to rest on a bench beneath the giant oaks in Bienville Square. He would sit there smoking his pipe and savoring the events of his day among the ships.

The visits to the waterfront, however, gave the Captain only temporary solace. He tried to occupy himself at home, puttering about in his garden, but somehow weeding and pruning and transplanting were only dull, meaningless tasks, and after an hour or so of gardening he would sit on a bench under the tree and smoke his pipe and gaze into space.

People who lived nearby no longer attempted to be

Sometimes his homesickness for ships and water exerted a pull as strong as the tide itself.

friendly or even bothered to speak when they passed. Occasionally someone would comment on the Captain's increasing gauntness and on the look of trapped agony in his eyes, but others would retort, "Well, if he would even be halfway friendly he wouldn't be so lonesome. He acts like he thinks he's too good to associate with us. So let him alone!"

Early one morning the Captain left home, smoking his pipe and wearing his cap proudly, as a ship's officer should. He spent the day wandering around the wharves admiring the ships and chatting with the sailors about happenings on their latest voyages. At the end of the day he gave his customary farewell salute to a departing freighter and went home, pausing on his way to spend a little while watching the fish swim around in the basin of the bronze fountain in Bienville Square.

People who met him on this return trip said later that he had a resolute and determined air about him, the look of a man who had made a decision after a long period of wretched uncertainty.

The neighbors saw the Captain go into his house. In a few minutes they heard the sharp crack of a shot followed by the sound of someone falling downstairs. When they forced their way into the house, they found his body lying at the foot of the staircase, a pistol clutched in his hand and his captain's cap still on his head. Beside his body lay his pipe, warm from his final smoke.

Some time after the Captain's suicide, Charles Smallwood, an Englishman, bought the house on State Street, and at his death the property went to his son, William Smallwood.

It was after the William Smallwood family moved into the house that the visitations of the Captain's ghost began.

One night Mr. and Mrs. Smallwood were awakened

by a loud noise that sounded as if someone had fallen down the stairs. Mr. Smallwood was certain that one of his sons had tripped in the dark and tumbled downstairs, but he found them sound asleep in their beds. Nobody—nothing—was on the stairs.

After they were awakened for several nights by the disturbance and after they failed to find any explanation for the bumps and thuds, Mr. and Mrs. Smallwood accepted the theory offered by the neighbors that the mysterious noises were caused by the Captain's ghost who was doomed to return and reenact his suicide as punishment for taking his own life.

As time passed the Captain's ghost began to supplement his nocturnal noises with daylight strolls around the yard. Mrs. Smallwood was terribly frightened one morning to see a strange man walking among her flowers, and her fright turned to terrified amazement when the man slowly vanished as she stared at him.

When she told the neighbors about this experience and described the intruder to them, they assured her that the description fit the Captain perfectly, even to the cap on his head and the pipe in his mouth.

This ghost not only made uncanny noises at night and was visible by day, but he also possessed another disconcerting quality: his presence was marked by the strong odor of tobacco being smoked in a pipe.

Often when Mrs. Smallwood was busy in the house, there would come drifting in from the backyard the unmistakable aroma of tobacco smoke. After a couple of confirming sniffs, Mrs. Smallwood would go swiftly out the back door and around the corner of the house, sure that she would catch her sons indulging in the evil habit of smoking.

"Willie! Willie! Where are you boys? Don't try to hide from me. I know you're out here smoking—I smell the tobacco. Come here this minute," the irate mother would order.

But although the odor of tobacco smoke grew heavier and heavier, nobody came and nobody answered.

Once in her search for the smokers she glimpsed a nautical cap vanishing into a clump of trees. And once as she was ordering the boys to step forth like men and confess their misdoings, she heard a deep chuckle followed by a salty oath.

The Smallwoods, though upset by these episodes, would likely have continued to live on State Street if the Captain had not begun annoying their cook, who was one of the best in Mobile.

Mrs. Smallwood knew that her cook was extremely afraid of the spirit world, and she had tried to keep her from learning of the Captain's ghostly visits. But one morning the cook came running into Mrs. Smallwood's room, trembling so that she could barely speak.

"A man wearing a funny cap has been standing in the kitchen door," she mumbled, "and when I asked him what he wanted, he just went away. He didn't walk off like folks—he just sort of melted away a little at a time."

Mrs. Smallwood tried to calm the woman by telling her that she had only imagined seeing the stranger. Her servant, still trembling, reluctantly returned to the kitchen —and there stood the Captain again!

This time all of Mrs. Smallwood's persuasive powers could not entice the cook to stay. Her highly prized servant did not stop to listen or even pause long enough to get her hat and coat. She dashed out the door and was never seen again.

Mrs. Smallwood's own nerves had almost reached the breaking point. The frequent appearances of the old sailor and the penetrating smell of his pipe had become unendurable.

As soon as they could find another house, the Smallwoods moved out, leaving the Captain in undisputed possession of the premises. For years afterwards the dwelling remained untenanted, save for the gloomy pipe-smoking ghost who could not take leave of the place where in lonely desperation he had put an end to his earthly existence.

Sturdivant Hall was one of the most splendid homes in the entire Black Belt.

The Return of the Ruined Banker

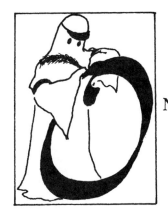NE AFTERNOON NOT LONG ago a guide was showing a group of tourists through Selma's Sturdivant Hall. The visitors had been given a brief history of the mansion from the time of its construction in 1852, and after admiring graceful proportions of the downstairs parlors they were guided to an upstairs bedroom.

It was here in the quiet of this corner room that the guide, while describing the rope-laced trundle bed and other old furnishings, suddenly stopped in mid-sentence. The guests noticed that she had become very pale, and one of the men in the group started to help her to a chair, but before he reached her she took a deep breath and continued her interrupted story.

After the tour was over and the visitors had gone, the guide hurried to her friend who was keeping the guest register.

"He's here again!" she exclaimed. "He brushed against me in the upstairs bedroom. I never felt anything quite

like it—his touch was clammy and frightening.

"And just last week," she exclaimed, "he was in the downstairs parlor. I'll never forget how that sudden rush of cold air felt! It seems he always comes when there are groups of tourists here. I can't decide whether he dislikes having strangers in his home or whether he wants to remind me to tell the people his remarkable success story and what a fine person he was. Whatever the reason, I know John Parkman's ghost is right here in Sturdivant Hall!"

80

John McGee Parkman lived in the white-columned mansion now known as Sturdivant Hall for only three years, 1864-1866, but they were three of the happiest years of his life.

At the age of twenty-nine, Parkman was president of The First National Bank of Selma, a new institution with a capital of one hundred thousand dollars; he had a charming wife and two beautiful little daughters, Emily Norris Parkman and Maria Hunter Parkman; he occupied a place of esteem in the social and business life of Selma; and his home was one of the most splendid in the entire Black Belt.

Life was good.

Then, with a suddenness that shocked the entire community, John Parkman's career ended in disgrace.

The youthful bank president was the victim of the same error of judgment that ruined older and more experienced businessmen during the postwar period: he speculated in cotton. Soon after he had invested large sums of the bank's money in cotton, the price of the fiber dropped from thirty and thirty-five cents to fifteen and eighteen cents per pound, and Parkman's bank lacked the funds to cover the losses.

Because federal money was deposited in The First National Bank, General Wager Swayne, commanding officer of the United States troops in the Selma district, moved in quickly, closed the bank, and placed Parkman under arrest.

Parkman was taken under guard to Cahaba and confined in Castle Morgan, the prison which had only a short time before been used by the Confederate government for the incarceration of Yankee prisoners.

Up to this point the facts about Parkman's life are clear, but there are confusing and conflicting reports regarding what happened after his imprisonment, particularly what happened following his escape from the stockade at Cahaba.

According to one story, friends in Selma, men who

believed that Parkman's poor judgment did not merit such severe punishment, arranged for his escape from Castle Morgan.

They first bribed the warden of the prison to cooperate with them in carrying out the escape plan. Then they arranged for a steamer to be waiting at the Cahaba wharf, some fifty yards down the bluff from the prison, to pick Parkman up. The scheme called for a group of musicians dressed in gay costumes to march up and down in front of the stockade to divert the guards while Parkman climbed over the rear wall of the enclosure and then escaped by running down the bluff to the waiting boat.

Every detail of the planned prison break seemed perfect.

The costumed musicians were putting on a splendid show at the prison entrance, the warden had left Parkman's cell unlocked, and the boat was waiting. But someone saw Parkman as he was climbing over the wall and gave the alarm.

Several shots were fired. Some witnesses said Parkman was shot as he dived into the river. Others said he was so frightened by the shots that he dived under the boat and was killed by the big paddlewheel. Still others contended that he made good his escape.

There was even disagreement about who fired at Parkman. One report was that his so-called friends shot him to make certain that Parkman would never divulge information which would have linked them with the bank scandal.

These friends, one story relates, claimed his body in secret and, hidden by the thick shrubbery, buried it at night near a scuppernong arbor at the rear of Sturdivant Hall.

Another more romantic but less plausible story says

that the young man's body was swept by the current down the Alabama River and that it finally lodged in the low limbs of a willow tree. It was the same tree, this story states, whose limbs had broken the window in their stateroom when Parkman was bringing his bride up the river from Mobile to Selma aboard a luxury river steamer.

If there are questions concerning Parkman's death, there is little question regarding the return of his ghost to his beloved Sturdivant Hall. Students of the supernatural say the ghost came back to try to clear Parkman's name of the blemish cast on it by his handling of the bank's funds, and perhaps their theory is right.

He did not return to Sturdivant Hall immediately after his death. In fact, it was not until after his home had been sold to Emile Gillman, about three years after the Castle Morgan episode, that Parkman's ghost first visited the premises. The property for which Parkman had paid sixty-five thousand dollars when he purchased it in February 1864, brought only twelve thousand dollars when it was sold to Gillman, and the transaction left Parkman's family destitute.

Servants in the home, many of whom had been employed by Parkman, were the first to be aware that his spirit had returned. They refused to walk through the back lot near the carriage house after dark, and even during the daytime they avoided the shadowy area with its thick growth of fig trees and scuppernong vines.

"Mr. Parkman's there," they would answer when asked why they skirted around the back lot. "He's come back."

Three or four of them stoutly declared that they had seen Parkman walking about in the orchard. Others were equally firm in their assertions that they had seen him on the side portico leaning against the iron grillwork railing. And still others told of having seen him quite distinctly

It must indeed be the restless, troubled ghost of John Parkman.

gazing out from the cupola atop the house.

All of the servants who talked of having seen Parkman affirmed their belief that he was buried near the scuppernong arbor and that his restless spirit roamed from that grave. Even when they were told that Parkman was properly interred in the family lot in Live Oak Cemetery, they kept insisting, "Mr. Parkman is right here. He's buried under the fig tree by the arbor. And he's troubled and restless. Mighty restless."

It must indeed be the restless, troubled ghost of John Parkman that wanders through the spacious rooms and around the grounds of the home he loved, appearing only when crowds of people are present. Is he objecting to the intrusion of these strangers into his home? Is he trying to play again the role of gracious host to a gay gathering of guests? Or is he seeking a defender, someone who will clear him of the stigma that has marred his good name?

Invariably the hole under the tree where Sketoe was hanged is clean, as clean as if a brush broom or a pine top had swept it out.

The Hole That Will Not Stay Filled

NOBODY HAS EVER ACTUALLY seen the ghost of Bill Sketoe, but people going along the road from Newton near where the old bridge crossed the Choctawhatchee River can tell that the ghost has been there. Invariably the hole under the tree where Sketoe was hanged is clean, as clean as if a brush broom or a pine top had swept it out.

Even if the hole is heaped high with dirt every day, the dirt disappears during the night, and the next morning the hole is there again.

Bill Sketoe, whose ghost apparently keeps the hole cleaned out, was born in Madrid, Spain, on June 8, 1818. When he was a little lad he came with his father to Dale County and settled near Newton, a small town in the Wiregrass section of Alabama.

There were not many Spaniards in that part of the country, and some people were suspicious of foreigners. But Bill was a good boy who won the respect of his neighbors, and when he grew up he became a Methodist minister.

After he entered the ministry, Sketoe became known as "the Bible-reading preacher from Spain," and he was invited to preach at churches throughout the area. He was made pastor of a log cabin Methodist church at Newton, and he was a kind pastor as well as a powerful preacher. It was while he was preaching at Newton that he met and married an attractive girl, and they built a home in the community.

Sketoe was made pastor of a log cabin Methodist Church near this Mount Carmel cemetery where he and his wife rest today.

When the Civil War began in 1861, Sketoe was one of the first men from his county to join the Confederate Army. He fought bravely for three years, being in the thick of many battles and miraculously escaping serious injury. Then in the fall of 1864 he received a message that his wife was very sick.

Having come from a country so far away from Alabama, Sketoe had no relatives to turn to for help. His wife did not have any close relatives either, at least not any whom Sketoe felt he could ask to stay with her in Newton to nurse her.

Sketoe decided that the only thing he could do was to hire a substitute to take his place in the Army so that he could go home to take care of his wife. It was not at all unusual for Confederate soldiers to pay other men to fight in their places during times of personal emergencies. The asking price for substitutes was about one thousand dollars, a lot of money for a rural Methodist minister turned soldier, but Sketoe somehow managed to scrape up the needed cash.

As soon as his substitute reported for duty, Sketoe jumped on his horse and headed for Newton, making the trip back home in near record time.

His wife was so glad to see her husband and so relieved to have him at home that she began to improve immediately. However, her long illness had left her weak and frail, and Sketoe felt he had to stay with her until she regained her strength.

The threat of defeat hung heavily over the South in 1864, and the Confederacy was in desperate need of every soldier it could get. Under these circumstances, Sketoe's prolonged stay at home began to arouse some resentment and suspicion. A few of his neighbors, who knew Sketoe was a foreigner, began to wonder if he might not be a traitor as well.

At Newton there were a number of men who had organized themselves to round up and punish deserters. They called themselves Captain Brear's Home Guard. There were some accusations that the Guard had been organized for the purpose of keeping its members safe at home while other men were away fighting for the South, but defenders of the unit said its members really were too old or too infirm to serve in the military forces and that they performed a commendable service for the Confederacy.

Be that as it may, the Guard heard about Sketoe's return from the Army, jumped to the conclusion that he was a traitor and laid plans to ambush him and give him a deserter's punishment.

On the evening of December 3, 1864, members of the Home Guard gathered at the foot of the bridge on the west side of the Choctawhatchee River to waylay their victim. When Sketoe appeared, two men engaged him in conversation, an apparent gesture of friendship to which Sketoe responded gratefully. He answered their questions about his wife's health and even showed them the medicine he had gone to town to purchase for her.

As they talked, the other men who had been hiding in a thicket of huckleberry bushes crept up behind Sketoe and slipped a noose of new rope around his neck. Sketoe was a big, strong man, but he was treacherously surprised. Although he struggled valiantly to escape, it was to no purpose. His arms were pinioned to his back by a tight cord, and his feet were tied together. Then his captors shoved him to the ground and took turns kicking him as they forced him to try to crawl in the deep sand.

Tiring of this sport and wishing to get on with the punishment they had planned, the members of the "military court" threw Sketoe into a buggy and maneuvered the vehicle to a spot underneath a stout limb jutting out from the south side of a big post-oak tree. This was to be Sketoe's hanging tree.

At this time Wesley Dowling, who knew and admired Sketoe, came down the road. When he saw what was happening, he stopped and began to beg the Home Guard to give their captive a fair trial. Instead of accepting this plea, one of the men gave Wesley a hard cuff and threatened to hang him too if he interferred further.

Alarmed lest other passers-by should see what they were up to, the men in the Guard hastened their preparation for Sketoe's hanging.

They threw the rope over the limb and then asked Sketoe if he had any last words. He replied that he would like to pray. This answer made the men a little uneasy, but how could they refuse to let a man have a final prayer, particularly if the man was a preacher? So they granted his request. Instead of praying for himself, as they had expected, Sketoe prayed for his tormentors.

"Forgive them, dear Lord. Forgive them," he prayed.

This prayer so infuriated the Home Guard that, even before the doomed man had finished praying, Captain Brear gave a sharp lash of his whip to the rump of the red horse hitched to the buggy. The frightened animal plunged forward, jerking Sketoe out of the buggy.

Sketoe's neck should have been broken, but in making their hurried plans for the hanging the Home Guard members had not allowed for their victim's height and size. Sketoe was tall, and his frame was not spare. So the limb to which the rope was tied bent under Sketoe's weight, and his toes touched the ground.

Quickly George Echols, a cripple, grabbed his crutch and used it to dig a hole in the sandy soil right under Sketoe's feet so that his toes could not touch the ground and his body would swing from the rope. The noose tightened and did its deadly work.

News of what was happening near the bridge reached Newton too late for friends to save the minister's life, but several men (among them Josh Morris, Dave Young, Bill Ard, and James W. Judah) went to the spot, took Sketoe's body down from tree, and laid it out in a cotton house across the road. He was later buried in the graveyard at Mount Carmel Church where his tombstone may be seen today.

But the story of Bill Sketoe did not end with his burial. The six men who had hanged Sketoe were never able to sleep peacefully at night, and not one of them would ever again walk alone outside after dark. Though they locked their doors and barred their windows, they were tormented by a nameless dread and fear. And each one in his turn met a violent death.

One was killed on horseback when a limb from a post-oak tree, the same kind of tree on which Sketoe was hung, fell on him. It was a still day, not a breath of wind stirring, but the heavy limb fell just as the rider passed beneath the tree. Another member of the lynch party was killed when thrown from a runaway mule that unaccountably took fright on a quiet, open stretch of road. A third member of the group was struck by lightning, and one was found dead in a deep swamp. The other two also met their deaths in mysterious ways.

Almost immediately after the hanging curious people began visiting the site of the tragedy. As time went by they observed that the hole dug by the crutch did not fill up as an ordinary hole would have done, and there were whisperings that Sketoe's ghost was returning to the spot to keep the hole clean.

Some years later two men who were part of a crew building a new bridge over the river decided to camp on

Quickly George Echols, a cripple, grabbed his crutch and used it.

the spot where Sketoe had died. They did not believe in ghosts, so they filled up the hole, pitched their tent over it, and the braver of the two men put his bedroll directly over the freshly-filled hole. They spent a fairly comfortable night.

Next morning when they broke camp the braver man picked up his bedroll and found to his amazement that the hole was there again although he had filled it up himself and had lain on it all night long!

It was a still day, but the heavy limb fell just as the rider passed beneath the tree.

The hanging oak is not there any more, but the hole is. It is about thirty inches wide at the top and slopes to a depth of about eight inches. Three young pine trees now grow close to the hole, but even their needles do not remain in it. Something sweeps them away, leaving the hole as clean and as empty as it was the day an innocent man was hanged there.

Pratt Hall at Huntingdon College has been haunted for years by a ghostly visitant known as the Red Lady.

The Red Lady of Huntingdon College

UNTINGDON COLLEGE in Montgomery has been haunted for years by a ghostly visitant known as the Red Lady.

Actually, according to some accounts, there have been two apparitions who walked or walk the dormitory halls by night and who wore or wear red.

The first lady dressed in red appeared at the college when it was still upstate in Tuskegee before moving to Montgomery in 1910. She was seen one night in Sky Alley, the top floor of the dormitory in the Tuskegee institution. It was just after all lights were turned off at ten o'clock in the evening when she came into view, walking up and down the corridors in lonely vigil.

Looking neither left nor right and uttering no sound, the lady clad in a red evening dress and carrying a red parasol was visible through a crimson aura of light which surrounded her and cast a lurid glow over her unearthly features.

The frightened students who saw her hastily gathered in one room and moved a heavy washstand against the door, but they continued to hear her footsteps. These weirdly rhythmic sounds alarmed them so greatly they became panic-stricken. One of the girls fainted, and nobody dared speak above a whisper until at dawn the tap, tap noise of her clicking heels died away and she was finally glimpsed disappearing in the gloom of an avenue of cedars leading to an entrance gate.

The students at the old college never saw the Red Lady again, but for a long time their sleep was made restless by memories of the ghostly promenade. The mind of one girl became so unhinged that she would not retire at all without having a lighted taper burning at her bedside, and the nerves of others neared the breaking point.

Nobody at Tuskegee could explain the reason for the appearance of this luridly red ghost in the college dormitory, nor did anyone know who she was; but there was a good reason for the visits of another Red Lady to the college after it was moved to Montgomery.

This ghost was a former student named Martha who had lived a sorrowful life which came to a tragic end in her room on the fourth floor of Pratt Hall. Martha was from New York, and she came to Huntingdon because her father's will specified that his daughter must attend her grandmother's—his mother's—alma mater. This alma mater had been Huntingdon when it was in Tuskegee. Martha did not especially want to come to Alabama, but her father's fortune was large and she knew his deep love for his home state of Alabama. So, although knowing no one in this deep-South area, Martha somewhat reluctantly came to Huntingdon. She was dressed in red when she arrived, and she brought with her red draperies for her windows and a red spread for her bed as well as other accessories of the same color. From

Looking neither left nor right, the lady clad in a red evening dress and carrying a red parasol was visible through an aura of light.

the beginning she refused to explain her apparent obsession with the color red.

Being a stranger and shy as well as unhappy in her unfamiliar surroundings, she could not make friends among the students. They sensed that she was different from themselves, and having heard she was wealthy they mistook her shyness for disdain.

Martha sat alone and apart from them in the dining hall. She seldom spoke to her roommate, and when girls dropped in to visit she seemed so cold and unfriendly they stopped coming. To tell the truth, many of them had come out of curiosity to see the red prayer rug Martha had bought in Turkey or the odd little red figurines on her bookshelves.

Her roommate found the situation unbearable and asked the housemother if she could move out. The housemother granted this request and put someone else in the room with Martha, who became increasingly aloof and irritable. This second girl also left her after only a week.

This procedure happened again and again as one roommate after another found it impossible to live with the surly girl. At last the president of the dormitory, who was known for her ability to get along with everybody, moved in with Martha and did all she could to make friends with her, but all efforts were futile. Martha had become embittered as well as withdrawn, and she seemed to resent the presence of this kindhearted girl.

After all her efforts at friendship had failed and after she found herself growing depressed and despondent, the dormitory president packed her belongings and prepared to leave.

Just as she was about to go, Martha, who had not known of her imminent departure, returned to the room.

With a look of defiance she said, "So you couldn't stand me either—like all the rest of your stuck-up friends. I was

beginning to think you really wanted me to be your friend
—but you hate me just like the rest. Well, I'm glad to be
rid of you! Take your things and go! But I'll tell you one
thing, my dear: for the rest of your life you'll regret leaving
this room."

The house president was disturbed by this bitter outburst, but in the midst of her many activities she soon forgot about Martha's prophetic words.

The sad girl, abandoned by the person she had believed to be her only friend, formed the habit of wandering into rooms where other girls were congregating, but her presence cast a chill upon the groups and they would soon find flimsy excuses for leaving her alone. Then with a feeling of alienation from all humankind she would return to her solitary sleeping quarters where she would wrap herself in her red bedspread as though she were retreating from the whole world.

Later her behavior became even more strange. She would wait until lights were out and then she would visit one dormitory room after another, never saying a word but staring into space as if she were in a trance.

As time passed, she took to walking up and down the halls during the darkest hours of the night. Often she would alarm girls by opening and closing their doors, then hurrying away to resume her pitiful promenade.

One evening after Martha had not appeared for classes or meals all day, her former roommate, the dormitory president, had a guilty feeling and decided to go to see her, thinking that this time she might be able to help Martha in some way.

As she neared Martha's room, at an isolated end of the corridor on the top floor of the building, she noticed the first of the now-famous flashes of red shooting out into the corridor, down from the room's transom as so many have since seen. She opened the door and screamed. Girls from all over fourth floor Pratt rushed from their rooms to see what was wrong.

They found the dormitory president lying in a faint within the doorway of Martha's room. Not more than three feet beyond her lay Martha, dressed in her red robe and draped in her red bedspread, with blood around her on the floor. Martha had carried out her threat by slashing her wrists and bleeding to death.

This happened a long time ago, but students at Huntingdon say that on the date of Martha's suicide each year rays of crimson light flash down from over her transom, and the Red Lady in her bizarre clothing returns to haunt the halls of Pratt Hall at Huntingdon College.

Purefoys still live here, as does a crying spirit from a covered well.

The Crying Spirit at the Well

 N THE LITTLE WILCOX County village of Furman, very few houses had waterworks during the 1800's. A good well, one that would not go dry during a long drought, was a highly prized possession.

But wells, even good ones, presented problems. Turning a heavy windlass over and over or tugging at a rope to draw up a bucket of water was hard work. Sometimes, especially in summer, there would be wiggletails swimming around in the bucket of water after it had been drawn up. Then the well had to be treated with salt to kill the wiggletails, and the drinking water had to be brought from a neighbor's well or spring. And things were always falling into wells—dippers, buckets, knives, sometimes even cats.

The worst thing that could happen to a well was for it to go dry. This is what happened at the home of Dr. John H. Purefoy, whose grandfather had been one of the early settlers of Furman, and whose Purefoy descendants live in the same house to this day. Dr. Purefoy had a large well in his back yard. The well went dry. There had been a parching hot summer with no rain for weeks, and not only this well but those of several neighbors dried up too.

This calamity occurred at a very busy time for Dr. Purefoy. Several of his patients were ill with malaria, and there were one or two babies ready to be born at any hour, so the busy doctor felt that he simply did not have time to cope with the problems of a dry well. He hoped that a heavy rain might replenish his water supply though he knew such a thing was quite unlikely.

To postpone the necessity of having a new well dug, Dr. Purefoy decided that water for use in the house and kitchen should be brought from a spring near Savage Hill, a mile or so down the sandy road, until the hoped-for rain renewed his well.

It seemed a simple solution. The spring produced the finest drinking water in the country, and its owner was quite willing to share his water with his friend the doctor.

Dr. Purefoy's servants, however, showed that they were not pleased with his plan. Dr. Purefoy thought that their dissatisfaction stemmed from having to make the inconvenient trips to the spring and back. He did not listen to their complaints closely enough to learn that it was not the trips that disturbed them. They were frightened by tales of the witch who guarded the spring.

Even if he had listened, Dr. Purefoy would not have been sympathetic. He did not believe in witches. So he was first displeased and then angry when his servants returned again and again from the spring with their buckets empty, damp but empty.

According to their stories, their trips were uneventful until they had filled their buckets with water and tried to go under or over the barbed wire fence that surrounded

106

A cat at the well had mean eyes.

the spring. The witch, they declared, was determined not to permit water to be taken out of the wired-in enclosure. No matter how hard they tried, the servants told Dr. Purefoy, the water always spilled when they reached the fence.

They were sure that the selfish witch at the spring caused the water to spill, but they could not convince the skeptical doctor of this fact. He tried to shame them for being superstitious, and when they attempted to tell him about the black cat at the spring, the cat with the mean eyes, he would not listen. However, even if he did not believe the tales about the witch, Dr. Purefoy was convinced that he could not depend on getting water from the spring and would have to get a new well dug in his own back yard. So he summoned a crew of Negro well diggers.

"I need a new well, and I need it as soon as you can dig it," Dr. Purefoy told them, and they nodded in agreement.

They nodded, too, when Dr. Purefoy cautioned them to use extreme care in digging in the sandy soil. He reminded them that the well might cave in on them and kill them.

"As you dig," he told them, "you must build a wooden casing inside the hole to keep the sides from caving in on you." He then showed them how to use the lumber and other materials they would need to build the casing.

Before they began to dig, one of the workers cut a slender forked branch from a peach tree to use to find the best place to dig. He held a fork of the Y lightly in each hand and walked slowly around the back yard. Soon the end of the branch began to twitch and jerk toward the ground. He stopped and shouted to the others, "Here's the place. Here's where the water is."

Then he marked the spot and they began digging.

Dr. Purefoy stayed with them until he was satisfied that the men would follow the safety precautions he had outlined. Then he drove off in his buggy to see his patients.

The well diggers followed his instructions for awhile, but building the protective casing slowed down their progress, and after they had dug down about ten feet they quit strengthening the sides with the wooden casing.

The work went faster then. They took turns going down into the excavation and shoveling dirt into the empty buckets which were pulled up by other workmen at the rim of the well.

It was growing late and they had decided to stop for the day when, suddenly without warning, the well caved in, completely covering the man who had been digging down in its bottom.

His companions worked frantically for hours trying to rescue him. Dr. Purefoy reached home shortly after the accident occurred, and he directed rescue efforts all night. As time passed, he knew that even if the body was recovered the man could not be revived, but his friends did not stop their efforts.

They continued digging for days, and occasionally they thought they heard faint cries for help coming from beneath the sand. But the body was never recovered. Some people believe it was sucked away by an underground current.

Nobody in Furman ever forgot the tragic death of the well digger for there appeared two remarkable and persistent reminders of it.

In the back yard behind Dr. Purefoy's house there is a slightly sunken area where the well was being dug. No grass will grow on this round spot.

Tenants who lived in a servant's house nearby told of a "black hant" that sat on the bare spot and cried all night

"Get me out of here. Please, please get me out."

long. They said his hot tears burned up the grass that tried to grow there and that he moaned bitterly as he cried.

And even those who had not ventured close enough to see the "black hant" told of having heard the plaintive cry, "Get me out of here. Please, please get me out," as they passed the Purefoy yard late at night. They recognized the words as the recurring death cry of the well digger, a ghost who continued to haunt the place where his life came to an untimely and horrible end when he was buried alive in Dr. Purefoy's well.

Grancer Harrison's tomb near Kinston is covered by a wooden, weatherbeaten shelter.

The Dancing Ghost of Grancer Harrison

HE TRIP INTO KINSTON HAD taken longer than the Coffee County farmer had planned, and he knew that no matter how fast the mules trotted it would be after dark before he and his family reached home. However, he reassured his wife, there would be a moon to light the road home, and the children could sleep on the pile of quilts in the wagon.

When his business was finished, he got the children settled in the back of the wagon, helped his wife up on the seat beside him, untied the mules from the hitching post, and headed for home.

As they rode along, the family finished eating the boiled peanuts they had bought in town. The children were quiet, but their father could hear them crunching on jaw-breakers. He hoped they would fall asleep soon—he did not want them to be awake when the wagon neared the Harrison Cemetery. Skittish mules, a frightened wife, and terrified children would be more than one nervous

113

man could handle if old Grancer Harrison's ghost chose to put on a performance.

He slowed the mules a bit to give the children more time to drift into slumber, and he tried to carry on a casual conversation with his wife. He knew what she was thinking: they had both heard stories that very afternoon of the dancing ghost of Grancer Harrison, and they dreaded passing his burial place.

By the time they had crossed the wooden bridge over Cripple Creek and had started up the hill on the other side, the children were asleep.

The farmer slapped the reins against the mules' broad backs and urged them into a trot. He wanted to get past the cemetery in a hurry.

The wagon had just reached the top of the hill beyond the creek and had come to a broad plateau when there began drifting toward the travelers the faint music of a fiddle playing "Devil's Dream" and the sound of dancing feet tapping out a rhythm to a lively tune.

The mules bolted. The woman clutched her husband's arm in panic. And from the back of the jolting wagon came sleepy voices asking, "What is it? Where's the dance?"

It was only after they had reached the safety of their own yard that the man turned to his wife and whispered, "Did you hear it too? Did you hear someone calling, 'Salute your partner'?"

She nodded. "Yes. I heard it all—the music, the dancing feet, the caller. All of it. It was old Grancer Harrison himself!"

This family was not the first nor was it the last to report an encounter with the lively ghost of Grancer Harrison, the "greatest dancer of them all." Just as Grancer's zest for living became a legend in southeast Alabama during his lifetime, so his ghost has become the area's most cele-

114

brated revenant.

Although the stories about Grancer are numerous, the facts about his life are sketchy. It is known that he moved to Coffee County from Virginia in the 1830's or early 1840's, bringing with him his family and his slaves. He homesteaded on land bordering the Pea River, the same river that in 1929 flooded and washed from the courthouse in Elba the records which would have substantiated the stories of Grancer's vast land holdings. On this land he homesteaded; at the edge of a high plateau overlooking the river he built his home.

Some people say Grancer Harrison built a mansion, a traditional Southern plantation house with wide porches, tall white columns, and tree-lined approaches. Others among his descendants say, despite his wealth, Grancer never built a fine house but lived in a simple one-story log house that had a wide dog-trot down the middle with rooms on each side.

Whatever the architectural style of his dwelling, it is agreed that Grancer Harrison's home was the social center of what is now Coffee, Geneva, and Covington counties.

His barbecues, with whole sides of beef roasting over beds of hot coals, his horse races (he reportedly brought with him from Virginia some "mighty valuable horse flesh"), and his dances attracted scores of guests to his home, and the amiable Grancer reveled in his role of host.

Perhaps to help offset reports that he cared only for entertainment and good times, Grancer excelled in farming. The yields of his long staple cotton were unmatched on any neighboring plantation, and growers came from miles around to get seed corn from him, hoping to duplicate his tall stalks, thick with full ears, which flourished in his bottom lands.

But though he took pride in his farming accomplishments and though he delighted in racing his fine horses and though nobody could match his appetite for barbecue, dancing was what he most enjoyed.

Almost every weekend he issued blanket invitations to his neighbors to come and dance to the music of his plantation band. If his friends did not know how to dance, Grancer taught them.

After awhile the number of guests at his dances grew so large his home could not accommodate them all. So then Grancer supervised the building of a large dance hall right in his yard. It was an immense structure, big enough for a hundred or more dancers. At one end was a raised platform for the musicians, and around the walls were benches for the spectators or for couples who wanted to sit and talk awhile. The floors were of hardwood, kept waxed and polished to a slick gloss by a team of servants whose sole duty was to care for the dance hall.

On weekends the place was filled with dancers. Often during the week, when there were no guests, Grancer would go to the dance hall with the fiddler from his band and would spend hours practicing the buck dancing and other intricate steps which so delighted his gallery of weekend spectators. He had special dancing shoes made for himself, and his tailor fashioned for him a handsome suit, somewhere between Sunday best and strictly formal wear.

Folks watching Grancer's flying feet used to laugh and say, "He sure stirs up a dust when he dances. Yessir, that Grancer purely dances up a whirlwind!"

The passing years did not decrease Grancer's love for dancing, but at last he realized that his frolicking days would soon end. He began to talk of death, not in a morbid way but with the practical approach of a businessman preparing for the inevitable.

"I want to be buried right here," he told his family,

116

Grancer's zest for living became a legend during his lifetime.

pointing to a spot only a few yards from his dance hall. "I want to be where I can hear those fiddles and feel the rhythm of the dancing feet."

Having selected his final resting place, Grancer began making other preparations. He sent his servants to Milton, Florida, to bring back a load of brick from the kiln there, and upon their return he set his skilled brickmasons to constructing his tomb. This tomb, all above ground, was unusually wide so that it could hold the featherbed on which Grancer wished to be buried.

The top of his tomb remained open awaiting his death, and a wooden pavillion was built over the burial plot to protect it from the weather.

His instructions were explicit. "When I die," he said, "I want to be dressed in my dancing clothes with my dancing shoes on my feet. Then I want to be placed on my feather-bed and carried to my tomb. After I've been laid in it, resting peacefully on my soft bed, I want my workmen to take the brick we saved for the purpose—they know where the bricks are stored—and seal the top.

"And the dancing must go on in my dance hall."

These instructions were carried out faithfully when he died, and for awhile the dances continued. But somehow the gatherings were not much fun without Grancer there to call the figures and to teach new dances and to stir up the dust with his fancy dance steps. Gradually folks quit coming, and the hall was seldom used.

It was soon after his friends stopped congregating in the dance hall that people going down the road near Grancer's tomb reported hearing a rollicking fiddle and dancing feet. These first stories brought scoffs of disbelief from listeners, but more and more people told of hearing old fiddle tunes and rhythmic tapping of shoes coming from

118

"When I die I want to be dressed in my dancing clothes with my dancing shoes on my feet."

the Harrison burying ground, particularly on Saturday nights.

Frequently horses and mules shied and bolted as they approached the place, and their drivers were certain that the animals, too, heard the sounds of the ghostly dance.

And those who heard it declared there was no doubt that the ghost of Grancer Harrison was dancing again, stirring up a dust, to the lively tunes he loved.

In recent years John A. Burgess of *The Opp News* has collected stories about Grancer Harrison and has compiled much information about this colorful Coffee County citizen.

Burgess often goes to the Harrison Cemetery near Kinston to visit Grancer's grave and to look out from the high plateau across the river valley and the gently rolling hills. Strolling along the plateau he tries to imagine where the Harrison home stood and what it looked like, and sometimes he tries to recreate in imagination the gay dances in Grancer's hall.

Burgess says he is not a real believer in the supernatural, but this is what happened to him:

One day he was out with his dogs in the vicinity of the Harrison Cemetery. It was a bright, sunny afternoon, still and cloudless. Burgess walked up the rise toward the cemetery and paused at the top to look out across the countryside and to wonder how many times Grancer must have delighted in the same magnificent view.

Thinking of Grancer, he turned toward the brick tomb. At that very instant, the sun disappeared behind a black cloud, and a cold gust of wind swept past Burgess. And in the cemetery, a swirl of dust danced from Grancer's sheltered tomb.

Afterword to the Commemorative Edition

In the mid-1960s—maybe because she had publishing friends in north Alabama, or maybe because she thought it would sell and she sure could use the money, or maybe just because she wanted to see if she was up to the challenge—Mother decided she would write a cookbook. *Treasured Alabama Recipes* became an instant big seller, largely because of the stories that accompanied the family collection of recipes.

Shortly after the release of the cookbook, Margaret Gillis Figh, one of Mother's college English professors, called her. "Kathryn, you are going to write another book, and this time it doesn't need to have any recipes in it. It needs to be a book of stories," Dr. Figh told her. "I'll be your collaborator if you like."

About this same time unexplained occurrences began in our house.

I was the only child still at home, my older sister and brother by then off at college. One afternoon Mother and I were in the kitchen rolling out cookie dough. Our house was small but big enough. The narrow kitchen immediately adjoined the small dining room, which opened through paned double doors into the living room.

That afternoon is indelibly imprinted in my memory. I'd floured the rolling pin and Mother had dampened the counter so the edges of the waxed paper wouldn't roll up. We'd sprinkled more flour on the waxed paper—when making cookies nothing should stick to anything else—and the lump of dough was plopped down and ready to roll out.

At that very moment we heard a ruckus in the living room unlike anything I've ever heard since: loud and scratching noises that seemed to come from not one particular area of the room, but rather from a room filled completely with the unsettling sound as though the midget demons of hell might have been turned loose all at once.

We looked at each other, startled, and moved to investigate. Mother wiped flour on her apron as she hurried to open the double doors into the living room. At the first movement of the doors the room became totally silent—no, eerily silent. I was right beside my mother, looking through the panes into the room. "What was that, Mama?" I asked her more out of curiosity than fear. She hesitated. "I have no earthly idea," she said finally.

We stood there for a minute before Mother dismissed it as a squirrel that might have fallen down into the fireplace, though there was no squirrel. There was nothing in that room except the furniture. We went back into the kitchen. As soon as the dough was almost thin enough to make acceptably crisp cookies, it began again, this time louder and with more force than before. And again, the minute Mother pushed the door, it all stopped. Not one item in the room was disturbed. Not one picture was crooked. Not one glass paperweight had fallen from the mantel.

Though Mother and I waited with some anticipation, the remainder of that day was quiet, ordinary. But in the weeks and months that followed, the unaccountable goings-on continued. They began with loud footsteps clumping down the hall, the steps ending abruptly just inside my brother's bedroom with a jarring slam of the door.

Subsequent strangeness took the form of furniture rearranging, not just shifting a bit as it would if a foundation was settling, but honest-to-goodness interior redecorating—beds rearranged to balance dressers moved from one wall to another. Freshly baked cakes flying—not falling, but *sailing*—off the dining room table. We were amazed, entertained, puzzled, but we were never frightened. My brother and sister pooh-poohed our stories on their first visits home from college. But as the unusual goings-on manifested themselves to my siblings, they, too, were intrigued.

DILCY WINDHAM HILLEY

↜

My mother was a multifaceted woman.

She taught a Sunday school class and made sure we went to church twice on the Sabbath. She was a believer.

She also was generous, perhaps to a fault. One Christmas we got extra stockings. As always, we drove down later to my grandmother's house in Thomasville, but Mother made an unexpected detour down a dirt road that she chose at random. We saw an African American woman walking with two small children. They were total strangers to us.

Mother stopped the car and asked me to give the children our extra stockings that were filled with candy, toys, and fruit. The children's mother's eyes sparkled.

"Santa Claus has come for you at the store and now he's come here," she told the children.

That was so like Mother. She told me about visiting a poor family with her father, who was a country banker, when she was young. She played in the dirt with the family's children that afternoon, and later she and her father shared in their meager evening meal.

"You're not better than they are," her father told her when they left. "You're just used to better things." She remembered the lesson all her life.

On the other hand, she believed in the supernatural.

I was skeptical of Jeffrey and her stories. Whenever someone asked me if I believed, my stock reply was, "Sure! Jeffrey sent me to college."

123

That always drew a laugh from the visitor and a wry smile from Mother.

One day, I was preparing to leave Selma for a job in New Mexico. My suitcase was packed and on my bed. Knowing that I had a long way to drive and that it would be many months before I saw Mother again, I embraced her in a lengthy good-bye hug.

Suddenly, my suitcase jumped from my bed, flipped over twice in the air, and landed beside me.

Mother and I just stared at each other.

"Jeffrey," she finally whispered. She wore the same wry smile.

I hit the road quickly. After that, I, too, was a believer.

BEN WINDHAM